WELCOME TO
PASSPORT TO READING
A beginning reader's ticket to a brand-new world!

Every book in this program is designed to build read-along and read-alone skills, level by level, through engaging and enriching stories. As the reader turns each page, he or she will become more confident with new vocabulary, sight words, and comprehension.

These PASSPORT TO READING levels will help you choose the perfect book for every reader.

READING TOGETHER
Read short words in simple sentence structures together to begin a reader's journey.

READING OUT LOUD
Encourage developing readers to sound out words in more complex stories with simple vocabulary.

READING INDEPENDENTLY
Newly independent readers gain confidence reading more complex sentences with higher word counts.

READY TO READ MORE
Readers prepare for chapter books with fewer illustrations and longer paragraphs.

This book features sight wo⋯ ⋯from the ⋯cator-supported Dolch Sight Words List. This ⋯ ⋯ ⋯cognize commonly used vocabular⋯ ⋯ ⋯ speed and fluency.

For more information, please visit passpor⋯⋯ ⋯com.

Enjoy the journey!

Little, Brown and Company

Hachette Book Group
1290 Avenue of the Americas, New York, NY 10104
Visit us at lb-kids.com

Little, Brown and Company is a division of Hachette Book Group, Inc. The Little, Brown name and logo are trademarks of Hachette Book Group, Inc.

The publisher is not responsible for websites (or their content) that are not owned by the publisher.

First Edition: April 2015

Library of Congress Cataloging-in-Publication Data

Belle, Magnolia.
Power Ponies to the rescue! / adapted by Magnolia Belle. — First edition.
pages cm. — (My little pony)
"Based on the episode 'Power Ponies' written by Meghan McCarthy, Charlotte Fullerton & Betsy McGowen."
Summary: "Spike and the ponies—Twilight Sparkle, Pinkie Pie, Fluttershy, Rainbow Dash, Rarity, and Applejack—are pulled into a comic-book world and must defeat an evil mare! Can they save the day?"— Provided by publisher.
ISBN 978-0-316-41085-4 (pbk) — ISBN 978-0-316-34200-1 (ebook)
I. McCarthy, Meghan. II. Fullerton, Charlotte. III. McGowen, Betsy. IV. Title.
PZ7.B4144Po 2015   [E]—dc23   2014041952

10 9 8 7 6 5 4 3 2 1

CW

Printed in the United States of America

Passport to Reading titles are leveled by independent reviewers applying the standards developed by Irene Fountas and Gay Su Pinnell in *Matching Books to Readers: Using Leveled Books in Guided Reading*, Heinemann, 1999.

Licensed By:

POWER PONIES
TO THE RESCUE!

Adapted by Magnolia Belle

Based on the episode "Power Ponies"

written by Meghan McCarthy,

Charlotte Fullerton & Betsy McGowen

LITTLE, BROWN AND COMPANY

New York   Boston

Attention, My Little Pony fans!
Look for these words when you read
this book. Can you spot them all?

comic

costumes

mailbox

lightning

Everypony is hard at work.
The friends are cleaning
Luna and Celestia's castle.

"Is there anything I can help
you with?" Spike asks.
"No, thank you!" Twilight says.

Spike finds a quiet place
to read his comic book.

Soon, the ponies look for Spike.

They want to share some snacks.

They find him reading a
secret message out loud.
"Take a closer look to join the
adventure in this book," Spike says.

The words are magic
and pull the ponies and
Spike into the book!

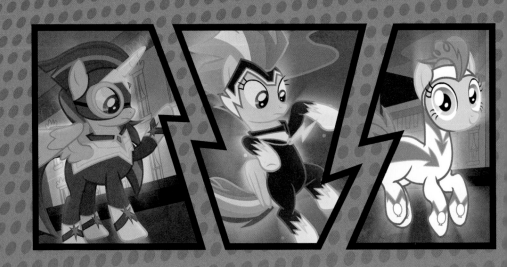

They are not in Ponyville anymore.
They are in a city called Maretropolis
and are all wearing costumes.
It is like they are inside Spike's
comic book.

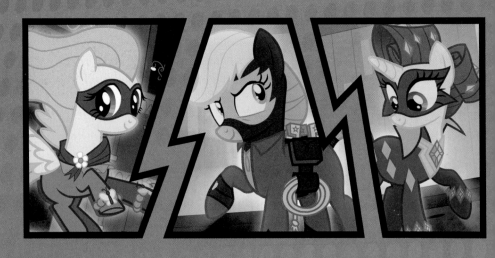

"You are the superheroes
from my comic book!
It zapped us here somehow!"
says Spike.

"Power Ponies!
You think you can
stop me?" asks the
crazy villain known
as the Mane-iac.

"Did she just call us Power Ponies?"
asks Applejack.

Spike knows the evil purple pony.
She is from his comic book.

"Somepony zap us back!"
shouts Rainbow Dash.
"The comic says the only way out is
to defeat the Mane-iac!" says Spike.

The Mane-iac wants to fight.
She uses her hair to throw things
at the Power Ponies.
Pinkie Pie runs from a mailbox.

She moves so fast,
the other ponies cannot see her.

WHERE DID PINKIE GO?

ZOOM

SHE IS THE FASTEST PONY IN ALL OF MARETROPOLIS.

The Power Ponies use their skills
against the Mane-iac.
Applejack tries to catch her
with a golden lasso.
Twilight tries to shoot a freeze ray
from her horn.

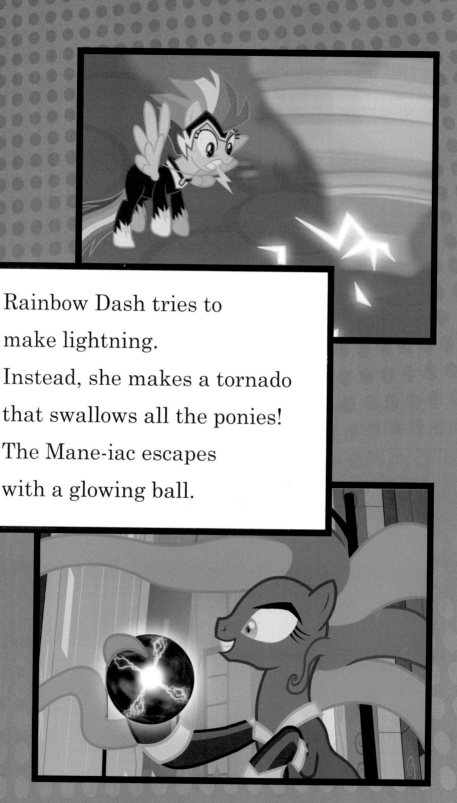

Rainbow Dash tries to
make lightning.
Instead, she makes a tornado
that swallows all the ponies!
The Mane-iac escapes
with a glowing ball.

"Oh no! The Mane-iac got away with the Electro Orb. She can use that to destroy Maretropolis," says Spike.

"No biggie.
We are awesome.
We have superpowers!"
says Rainbow Dash.

"I do not have any," says Spike.

Twilight reminds Spike
he is the only one who
knows Maretropolis.
He leads the team to the
Mane-iac's secret base.
"Is that a shampoo
factory?" Pinkie Pie asks.

"Come on out, Mane-iac, or the Power Ponies are coming in!" shouts Applejack.

The Power Ponies battle

the Mane-iac's henchponies.

The heroes are about to win.

Then the Mane-iac uses a secret weapon!

HAIR SPRAY OF DOOM

She stops all the ponies,
but she does not stop Spike.
"It would be pointless to spray
you," the Mane-iac says.

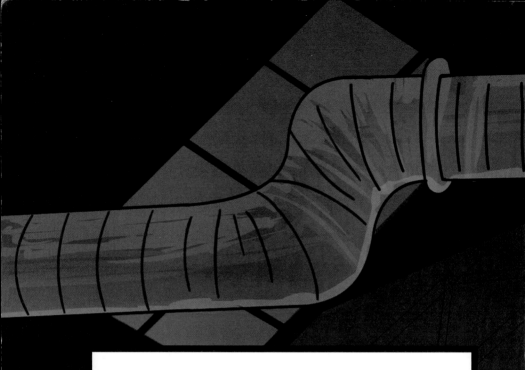

Spike sneaks into the Mane-iac's base through a vent.

"How am I supposed to help my friends?" he asks himself.

"This cannon will cause the mane of everypony in Maretropolis to grow wild," says the Mane-iac.

"Are you forgetting about somepony?"
asks Fluttershy.

The Mane-iac laughs and says,

"Little guy?

No superpowers?"

"He always comes through for us,"
says Twilight.

Twilight's words make Spike brave.
He distracts the Mane-iac's henchponies
and sets the Power Ponies free!

The Power Ponies then work together
to capture the crooks.
They can leave Maretropolis!

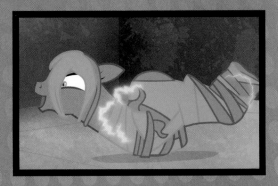

The friends celebrate in Ponyville.
"You do not have to have superpowers
to be a super friend," says Spike.
The friends all cheer and eat cupcakes.